SOME PIG'

SOME PIG!

A *CHARLOTTE'S WEB* PICTURE BOOK

BY E. B. White

ILLUSTRATED BY Maggie Kneen

HarperCollins*Publishers*

ℱERN LOVED WILBUR MORE THAN ANYTHING. She loved to stroke him, to feed him, to put him to bed. Every morning, as soon as she got up, she warmed his milk, tied his bib on, and held the bottle for him.

Every afternoon, when the school bus stopped in front of her house, Fern jumped out and ran to the kitchen to fix another bottle for him. She fed him again at suppertime, and again just before going to bed. Mrs. Arable gave him a feeding around noontime each day, when Fern was away in school.

Wilbur loved his milk, and he was never happier than when Fern was warming up a bottle for him. He would stand and gaze up at her with adoring eyes.

For the first few days of his life, Wilbur was allowed to live in a box near the stove in the kitchen. Then, when Mrs. Arable complained, he was moved to a bigger box in the woodshed.

At two weeks of age, he was moved outdoors. It was apple-blossom time, and the days were getting warmer. Mr. Arable fixed a small yard especially for Wilbur under an apple tree, and gave him a large wooden box full of straw, with a doorway cut in it so he could walk in and out as he pleased.

"Won't he be cold at night?" asked Fern.

"No," said her father. "You watch and see what he does."

Carrying a bottle of milk, Fern sat down under the apple tree inside the yard. Wilbur ran to her, and she held the bottle for him while he sucked. When he had finished the last drop, he grunted and walked sleepily into the box.

Fern peered through the door. Wilbur was
poking the straw with his snout. In a short
time he had dug a tunnel in the straw. Fern
was enchanted. It relieved her mind to know
that her baby would sleep covered up, and
would stay warm.

Every morning after breakfast, Wilbur walked out to the road with Fern and waited with her till the bus came. She would wave good-bye to him, and he would stand and watch the bus until it vanished around a turn.

While Fern was in school, Wilbur was shut up inside the yard. But as soon as she got home in the afternoon, she would take him out and he would follow her around the place.

If she went into the house, Wilbur went, too.
If she went upstairs, Wilbur would wait at the
bottom step until she came down again.

If she took her doll for a walk in the doll carriage, Wilbur followed along. Sometimes, on these journeys, Wilbur would get tired, and Fern would pick him up and put him in the carriage alongside the doll.

He liked this. And if he was *very* tired, he would close his eyes and go to sleep under the doll's blanket. He looked cute when his eyes were closed because his lashes were so long. The doll would close her eyes, too, and Fern would wheel the carriage very slowly and smoothly so as not to wake her infants.

One warm afternoon, Fern and Avery put on
bathing suits and went down to the brook for
a swim. Wilbur tagged along at Fern's heels.

When she waded into the brook, Wilbur waded in with her. He found the water quite cold—too cold for his liking. So while the children swam and played and splashed water at each other, Wilbur amused himself in the mud along the edge of the brook, where it was warm and moist and delightfully sticky and oozy.

Every day was a happy day, and every night was peaceful.

Wilbur was what the farmers call a spring pig, which simply means that he was born in springtime. When he was five weeks old, Mr. Arable said he was now big enough to sell and would have to be sold.

Fern broke down and wept. But her father was firm about it. Wilbur's appetite had increased; he was beginning to eat scraps of food in addition to milk. Mr. Arable was not willing to provide for him any longer. He had already sold Wilbur's ten brothers and sisters.

"He's got to go, Fern," he said. "You have had your fun raising a baby pig, but Wilbur is not a baby any longer and he has got to be sold."

"Call up the Zuckermans," suggested Mrs. Arable to Fern. "Your Uncle Homer sometimes raises a pig. And if Wilbur goes there to live, you can walk down the road and visit him as often as you like."

"How much money should I ask for him?"

"Well," said her father, "he's a runt. Tell your Uncle Homer you've got a pig you'll sell for six dollars, and see what he says."

Soon it was arranged. Fern phoned and got her Aunt Edith, and her Aunt Edith hollered for Uncle Homer, and Uncle Homer came in from the barn and talked to Fern. When he heard that the price was only six dollars, he said he would buy the pig.

The next day, Wilbur was taken from his home under the apple tree and went to live in a manure pile in the cellar of Zuckerman's barn.

In memory of my uncle, Johnny Ockleshaw,
who was more help and inspiration than he knew
—M.K.

Library of Congress Cataloging-in-Publication Data is available.
ISBN-10: 0-06-078161-0 (trade bdg.) — ISBN-13: 978-0-06-078161-3 (trade bdg.)
ISBN-10: 0-06-078162-9 (lib. bdg.) — ISBN-13: 978-0-06-078162-0 (lib. bdg.)

Designed by Stephanie Bart-Horvath
1 2 3 4 5 6 7 8 9 10 ❖ First Edition